DIESEL DOCTRINE

AND THE TEMPORARILY EMBARRASSED MILLIONAIRES

DIESEL DOCTRINE

AND THE TEMPORARILY EMBARRASSED MILLIONAIRES

NICK ULANOWSKI

Diesel Doctrine and The Temporarily Embarrassed Millionaires

First Edition

Paperback ISBN: 978-1-64669-553-9

E-book ISBN: 978-1-64669-523-2

Printed by Lightning Source.

Written by Nick Ulanowski

Edited by Lindsay Moore

Book design by Jorge Santiago, Jr.

10 9 8 7 6 5 4 3 2 1

Fuck you, Greg Mclemen!

This book is all your fault.

INTRODUCTION

I've known Nick since we were little kids. We grew up in the same neighborhood, went to the same school, and rode the bus together. We bonded over things like Batman, Pokémon cards, and movies. These are the typical things that kids growing up in the late 1990s and early 2000s would have been into. But Nick was never just into the typical, popular things that other kids were into. One of my earliest memories of Nick was when we were in the playground at recess, and he explained vampire lore and history to me in great detail. He also showed me a book on urban legends and conspiracies, and as a nine-year-old that had not yet been introduced to the internet, I found it endlessly fascinating.

I love horror movies, and I owe a lot of my appreciation for horror movies to Nick. As a kid, I was familiar with the popular horror films of that time. I wasn't particularly interested in things like the *Final Destination* movies or another *Friday the Thirteenth* or *Nightmare on Elm Street* sequel. But Nick opened my eyes to a whole new world of horror: things like old monster movies, Hammer studios films, and straight to VHS gems. There was a whole world of interesting stuff out there, and I just had to look for it. That's what being a friend of Nick is like. He's always glad to chat about the latest superhero movie or hit TV show, but he's just as likely to introduce you to an indie comic book you've never seen, or a song you've never heard before. Who knows, maybe he'll show you your next favorite horror movie.

Our friendship has changed and grown over the years. We haven't lived in the same state since we were eighteen, but we've remained good friends. We only see each other in person a few times a year, but we still frequently talk, and I always enjoy hearing what Nick has to say. One of the things I have always admired about Nick is his ability to view things from different perspectives. We frequently talk about the movies we've seen, the shows we're watching, and the comics we're reading. I always leave our conversation learning something new or appreciating something that I had previously overlooked.

I'm glad I got to read *Diesel Doctrine*. Of course, the book is a work of fiction, but Nick has drawn from his own truck stop experiences and his unique perspective to bring this truck stop to life. I'm sure many of us have stopped at a truck stop at some point in our lives, either to fill up on gas, to grab a snack, or to take a break while on a long road trip. A lot of people probably don't think much about the people that work there, or what it must be like to spend a significant portion of your life there. *Diesel Doctrine* shows us what it must be like to devote so much time to working at a truck stop, the types of people you might encounter there, and the crap you would have to deal with. I'm sure many of you reading this have worked at jobs where the pay is too little, the scheduling is insensitive, and the rules and workplace politics make little sense. You might relate to having your life thrown out of balance after working repeated overnight shifts, or getting hours drastically cut despite years of commitment and hard work. The story gives us a great example of how so many workers in our country are undervalued, underappreciated, and underpaid for what they do.

So, clean up some shit, clock out, grab a prepackaged sandwich, crack open an energy drink, and read the book. Spend some time in Mitch's shoes, and learn the Diesel Doctrine, motherfucker.

Ed Kolkebeck
Columbia, Missouri
August 23rd, 2019

TABLE OF CONTENTS

CHAPTER 1
BACK ON THE GRIND

"You're late, Mitch."

"Fuck off, Calvin."

I walked past the fuel desk and into the restaurant to clock in. Technically, I was on time according to what the schedule said. But we're supposed to arrive fifteen minutes early and leave fifteen minutes late to cover our half-hour unpaid break. I had been up until 2AM the previous night on my computer. I didn't want to go to sleep and wake up and have to come to this fucking place again.

My name is Mitchell Derrick, and I've been working at a truck stop for way too fucking long.

"Hey, Mitch!" said Kelly. I forced a smile, said hi, and walked out of the restaurant into the store and into the janitorial closet where I got dressed.

Before I even had my smock on, I heard on the intercom, "MITCH to the office, Mitch to the office," in a very angry tone. It was the fucking new general manager Cindy. She transferred here about a month ago and she replaced Craig, the guy who hired me.

When Cindy first got here, I was constantly undressing her with my eyes. She was a red-headed biker chick in her mid-thirties and had tattoos on her neck. But now I just thought the bitch was gross, constantly yelling at people, swearing and threatening to fire people. She also doesn't know how to fucking talk. It's one thing to speak a certain way colloquially in a casual manner, but I really think she just doesn't know proper grammar at all.

She once actually said to a truck driver and regular customer here, "so, you ain't never seen no chick with no cigarette today?"

What the hell does that even mean? Is she asking if he's seen a bunch of women with cigarettes or is she asking if she was supposedly the first and only one? I think it means that I work for a backwoods shmuck who does a good job of raping the English language. And apparently this is who gets to run the place now.

I put on my smock and walked out of the janitorial closet, out of the men's bathroom and over to the manager's office. The door was closed. I have about seven keys for this job but not one of them opens up this particular door. I knocked. I waited about twenty seconds, but there was no response. I knocked again, this time harder. I waited for another minute, but there was still no response.

What the fuck? Another day, another fucking dollar.

I walked to the back of the store and grabbed an energy drink to purchase. I then walked back to the fuel desk and said, "Calvin, can you page Cindy to the fuel desk?"

"Sure thing, boss," he replied. Calvin was the self-proclaimed "office asshole" around here. A lot of my co-workers have a real problem with him. I think he's the best thing to happen to this truck stop since sliced bread; or perhaps the best thing since those pre-packaged chicken and cheese sandwiches that cost a little over two bucks.

Calvin picked up the phone behind the counter. His voice behind the fuel desk and above me over the intercom said, "welcome to Petrol. Cindy to the fuel desk, please. Cindy to the fuel desk." He hung up the phone. I set my energy drink down on the fuel desk, and he rang it up for me.

"So, Calvin, how was Mexico?" I asked.

CHAPTER 2
CALVIN'S PROMISED LAND

In the film *Men in Black 2*, it's said that most people who work at post offices are aliens from outer space. Well, I think most of the people who work at and patronize truck stops are aliens as well.

Take Calvin, for instance. This particular truck stop has a predominately white workforce and is located on the fringes of a predominately black suburban area and the rural Midwest. In this environment, Calvin was a cultural freak – a short, sarcastic Hispanic dude hailing from a small town just outside of a large metropolitan area. He was born here in the U.S., but took great pride in being of Mexican descent. He spent much of his childhood living in Mexico. So far, this is nothing particularly abnormal. Mexican-Americans are everywhere. What made Calvin a special case study was his viewpoint of returning to Mexico as some kind of Promised Land. As he put it, "it'll be great. I'll be the only asshole American there."

Calvin claims he was once a nice guy but working at Petrol turned him into an asshole. He has taken pride in waging "wars" with other co-workers and stirring the pot when office drama ensued. He stuck up for me on several occasions and talked shit about me on others. I considered him a friend, but for many others at the truck stop, he was an annoyance. In the end, he always made the place much more interesting.

After getting his bachelor's degree, he decided to quit Petrol and move in with a few family members in Mexico. He wanted to go to school there, start his own business, and seek a better life. He returned months later, talking about what a horrible place Mexico was and how he never wished to return. He said the school he attended was over-run by the heirs of people involved in the drug trade. He said this was because these people were almost the only people in Mexico who could afford such a school. He said the laws were fascist and he called the country uncivilized. He returned to America talking about how he was proud to be an American. As everyone of all creeds and colors said to Calvin upon his triumphant return, "well, duh. Why the fuck do you think so many people are fleeing Mexico?"

And alas, he returned to America and to Petrol as a lowly cashier after having left this job and this country as a shift lead. Everyone but me was happy to see him as a cashier and not in a position of power. Even Calvin himself was satisfied because he was an educated man who hoped to leave Petrol for a better job as soon as possible.

I suppose Calvin understood what I like to call "Diesel Doctrine" better than anyone here. He was the opposite of everything I distained about the truck stop. Yet, as both an outsider and in part an insider, he understood the culture of this place very well. He knew how things worked around here, even if some perceived him as a trouble maker.

This is the same guy who once invited me to come with him to the Occupy protests downtown. Some redneck truck driver overheard and said to him, "you come to this country and you protest America. Go home. Just go home."

I laughed and said, "yeah, Calvin, go home. Clock out early and go home to your apartment down the street."

Good old Calvin. He was always one of my favorite people at the truck stop but far from the only one of us who was more than just a little fucked up in the head.

CHAPTER 3
WORKER ANTS

"It's funny because I think it's possible to live it up while working at this place, but even a general manager doesn't even come close to living large."

Holt looked up from scrubbing the shit stains off the shower room wall and replied, "what's the fucking difference?"

I replied, "well, you can live it up in a Section 8 apartment or your mother's house but, by definition, you're not living large if that's your living arrangement. Similarly, you can live it up with a seven-hundred-dollar car stereo system, but you ain't livin' large if it's in a ten-year-old Ford Focus."

Holt and I have been friends since high school. He was a junior and I was a freshman when I first met him. We had mutual friends back then and still do to this day. I consider him one of my best friends and his being here is one of the few perks of working at Petrol. I actually got Holt the job. I recommended him, brought him into work and he was hired on the spot.

The job opening was created after a porter named John died

of a heart attack. John was an ex-trucker in his fifties who ate way too much greasy food, I guess. The XXXL-sized smocks he was given weren't big enough, so he wore his work shirt unbuttoned. He had too much truck stop food and not enough exercise while driving around all year in a truck, I suppose. He was only in his fifties and his arteries weren't healthy enough for him to live any longer. The man died hours before he was scheduled to come in to work an overnight shift.

I got a text from the general manager Craig about John's death. Because he was dead, he was unable to come to work that day. I came in to cover his shift and pick up some overtime. A week later, I attended his memorial service and spoke to his son, John Junior, and the rest of his family. At the service, I grabbed a copy of the photograph of John they were handing out in bulk. The next morning, I brought it to work and stuck it on the bulletin board in the janitorial closet. You could say that this place fucking killed him, and I made money from his death.

John was apparently friends with Fred, another porter who works here. This was partially how he got the job. John Junior had also been a porter at Petrol and was in his early twenties, a few years younger than me.

John Junior quit Petrol after a dispute with me. He came in to work overnight and complained about some of the downstairs bathrooms being dirty. Like me, his job was to clean the bathrooms. I had been busting my ass cleaning shower after shower as customers purchased them. Quite frankly, the overnight porter's job is to take care of the work we didn't get around to doing. Nonetheless, John Junior took pictures with his smart phone of the dirty bathroom and showed Craig the next morning.

Craig's response was, "well, it's your job to clean up that shit."

Despite Craig's solidarity with me, I had a word with John Junior in private about it the next time I saw him. I told him, "if you don't like cleaning bathrooms, then don't fucking work here."

He was dead silent as I spoke. He quit the next day. Later on, I spoke to John Junior at his father's memorial service and he ironically gave me a hug and claimed I had nothing to do with why he quit. This doesn't change the official story if you ask anyone who worked at Petrol.

Rumors spread like wildfire at the truck stop, and many people have outside connections with other employees. Everyone was in everyone's business. Perhaps this was a part of the "Diesel Doctrine".

Anyway, all of that happened almost a year ago. It was almost five o'clock as I continued to converse with Holt off the clock. I had worked 8AM to 4PM, and he was my relief, working the 4PM to midnight shift. It was never a problem for Holt. He enjoyed my company. However, management was growing weary of this and felt it wasn't the best idea for maximizing work potential. Neither the general manager nor the assistant manager were here right now, but the shift lead was. I was talking with Holt about our mutual friends from outside work while he folded towels when Brad, the shift lead, walked into room. Brad smirked.

"Mitch, what are you doing?" he asked teasingly.

What is a shift lead? A shift lead is a glorified cashier, and I mean that in the most respectful way possible. A shift lead is our boss, for sure. However, he's only here on a Friday night because the assistant manager and general manager don't want to be here. The shift lead does the dirty work, the grimy shit that the real bosses don't want to do. If something goes wrong, it's not a manager's fault, it's the shift lead's fault. A shift lead is a whipping boy. A shift lead takes the blame, works the shitty hours and does the menial managerial tasks. A typical day in the life of a shift lead sucks, but at least they get paid enough to afford a cheap apartment. I don't – at least, not if I care to pay any other bills.

Brad was a young, white, male transplant from Arizona. He wasn't used to this cold weather at all. During the winter time, he never whined, even though it would've been a legitimate complaint. Brad was one of the most easygoing guys I knew. For a guy in a position of power, he's really chill. Brad is the only boss I've ever had who I've never wanted to punch in the face. As Holt and I always said, "Brad should just run this place."

All that said, he was somewhat of a pushover. I don't mean he was a pushover with his employees, but with his bosses. Ultimately, this made me angry at the place, not him. I knew he was just doing his job and following orders from higher-ups. It always seemed like he was more competent than the higher-ups, but he remained a shift lead year after year. I felt like this was a dead-end job and ironically, I could turn to Brad and feel like he was in the same boat. It was a boat filled with bullshit. We said "yes, sir!" as we sailed around, and they continued to pile more and more bullshit onto us. But I guess you got to do what you got to do to survive.

Brad, his sister and his mother moved here from across the country after his father was put away for seven years in Arizona State Prison for trafficking narcotics. Brad's sister, Kelly, was a waitress at the Boiling Pan, a truck stop restaurant adjacent to Petrol. Brad's mother was disabled and collected SSI checks every month. She lived with Brad in his apartment, where he paid 100% of the rent. Brad dropped out of a nearby high school, and he has worked at the truck stop since he was eighteen. Brad and I actually knew each other back in high school. I used to party with a group of people from that suburban town and Brad was one of them. He wasn't a significant person to me back then. I just remember he was there. I worked here for about six months before realizing we had been previously acquainted. Now he's an important person in my work life.

"Just discussing business with Holt," I replied.

Brad tapped his wrist as if he were wearing a watch and said, "it's five o'clock. You know you aren't supposed to be here. Come on, man."

"Okay, will do."

Brad walked out the laundry room as Holt silently continued to fold towels. I grabbed my backpack and told Holt I'd see him tomorrow.

This always angered me. This is a public place, and I guess because I'm an employee, they called it "loitering". Truck drivers hang around the truck stop for days on end and we call them "customers" – even if they aren't spending money. But God forbid an employee hangs around for an extra hour off the clock to talk to people. Oh well. I could complain, but in the end, there was no point. Brad was the only person in a position of power that listened to any grievances of mine and in this instance, he was doing as he was told. I was a powerless worker ant in the colony that is this company. And there was nothing I could do about it but move where they told me to and obey.

CHAPTER 4
1-800-EAT-SHIT

I wasn't whistling as I worked, but that Zero Down song was stuck in my head again – the one about roads and bill collecting callers. I hummed it to myself as I wiped the water off the wall and cleaned the semen off the shower room floor. Fortunately, no one was waiting for a shower, but until I finished cleaning this one, there would be no showers available either. I quickly prepared the shower for the next customer, so he or she wouldn't have to wait.

Just as I was putting the shower back in service, I heard over the PA system, "welcome to Petrol. Porter to the fuel desk, please. Porter to the fuel desk." What the fuck? I'm the only porter working. Melissa could at least address me by name.

When I was first hired to work here, I worked the overnight shift five nights a week. It sucked, but at least I had weekends off back then. As I gained unofficial seniority, I no longer had to work overnights. However, for some time, I was working all three shifts during a five-day work week. These days, I only work the day shift and the evening shift. It's either a Thursday through Monday schedule or a Friday through Tuesday schedule. And I work 4PM to 12AM the last day or two of my work week.

It's nice to be able to work the evening shift after three or four days of working day shifts. I'm a bit of a night owl. I lose a lot of sleep while working the 8AM to 4PM shift for three or four days. But on that third or fourth day where I don't have to be at Petrol until 4PM, I can catch up on sleep. And this gap of time can allow me to mentally prepare for activities on my two days off instead of just being exhausted. And I never make the decision to stay home on the weekends just because I have work in the morning; I usually get to sleep by 2AM.

Melissa usually only worked the day shift, but she was covering a call off tonight. Melissa was in her late twenties and had three children. She lived at home with her mother, who helped her raise these children. She gave birth to one of her kids while she was working here at the truck stop. She had her first kid in high school and she's proud of having finished high school while raising this kid. A woman who isn't as strong as Melissa may have dropped out. She was indeed one of the few people here at Petrol who had graduated high school. High school graduates like me and her were like that United States Marines recruiting slogan – "the few, the proud."

I rushed downstairs to the fuel desk.

"What's up?" I asked.

"There are a few drivers outside illegally parked. Can you go outside and write down their truck number?"

This happened every night. I guess there aren't enough parking spaces at the truck stop for all the truck drivers on the road. So, out of desperation, they park in areas of the parking lot that aren't parking spaces and block other drivers from being able to pass through. It might suck that they can't find a place to park, but it's not our problem – or at least, it's definitely not the problem of low-level employees at the truck stop. These truck drivers illegally parked wouldn't like it if they were the truck driver who was trying to pass through.

I replied, "I'm really busy right now."

Before Melissa could reply, Calvin walked over from stocking the shelves and said, "suit up, man."

Melissa rolled her eyes. She seems to do that whenever Calvin says anything at all. Calvin was referring to the orange Road Crew vests we're required to wear whenever we walk outside. The vests were similar to what construction guys wear and served the purpose of increasing our visibility, so cars or trucks don't run over us.

Calvin handed me the Road Crew vest and I put it on.

He said, "if these assholes don't listen to us, write down their truck numbers so we can report them to their company."

Melissa printed out a blank receipt paper and handed it to me. I got a pen from behind the fuel desk. Calvin and I walked outside. He lit up a cigarette as we approached one of the idling trucks.

With Calvin behind me, I hopped onto the step right below the driver's side door of the truck. I knocked on the window. I waited about ten seconds and there was no response. I knocked again. There was still no response. I proceeded to walk over to the side of the truck and began writing down their company name and truck number. Just as I was in the middle of writing it down, the driver's side window flew open. I saw a black man in about his thirties with long dreads like Bob Marley.

"Excuse me, can you please move your truck to a designated parking area?" I asked.

"What? I been here three hours," he replied.

"Well, you've been illegally parked for three hours then."

He shut his window and remained parked. I went back to writing down his truck number.

Just as this is going on, I overheard a fat, middle-aged, white man telling Calvin, "Hey, you want my phone number too? It's 1-800-Eat-Shit!" Calvin just laughed.

The truck driver by me then opened his door and got out of his truck. He walked toward me standing tall with his chest out.

"I'm callin' corporate on your ass. What's your name?"

"I'm sorry, sir. But if you don't move, we're reporting you to YOUR company."

"You lookin' for a punch in the face?"

I stepped back. Calvin pointed towards the door. We had the truck numbers and company names, so without speaking another word, we walked back to the fuel desk.

"Where ya going, Ren and Stimpy? Come back here!" I heard the Jamaican-looking dude yell at us as we walked away. Neither of the drivers followed us, nor did they move their trucks for the rest of the night.

"We don't get paid enough for this shit," I said as I opened the front door.

Why no one bothered calling the cops on these illegally parked trucks, I will never know – not the assistant manager, not the shift lead and no one at the fuel desk. It would've made too much sense, I guess.

CHAPTER 5
TEMPORARILY EMBARRASSED MILLIONAIRES

"I be workin' 12 to 8 like a motherfuckin' owl
I'm like Batman but no cape or cowl
Instead I got a mop and a big set of keys
Slangin' KI's to the truckers? Yo, mind ya bees!
I'm a porter at Petrol, man, it ain't no joke
I can't wait to clock out and go home for a toke."

It was around 3AM. The morning rush wasn't to be expected for several hours. I was just hanging around in front of the fuel desk and freestyling with Sid. Because it was overnight shift, there wasn't a single other employee in the Petrol store. Sid sat behind the fuel desk with his MP3 player out, playing a beat from a popular hip-hop song as I rapped to it.

A truck driver was loudly snoring nearby as he sat in the chair inside the arcade. This was presumably more comfortable than sleeping in his truck. Sleeping inside the truck stop was technically against the rules, but we honestly didn't care. And it was unlikely that any assistant manager, general manager or shift lead checking the surveillance camera tomorrow was going to say anything. If they did say something to us about it, it would most likely just be an excuse to reprimand us because they were mad about something entirely different. An unwritten rule at the truck stop is that between the hours of 1AM and 6M, loitering and public sleeping is essentially allowed. Any written rules against these practices are simply not enforced in the dead of night.

When Craig first hired me, I was ecstatic to finally be working again. We're in a recession and it's tough out there. Jobs are hard to come by. And not only was I finally hired somewhere but I was working full time and earning more than minimum wage. But now, keeping these kinds of hours has started to take a toll on my mental health – and possibly even my physical health. Working overnight shift has got me all kinds of fucked up.

It's ironic. I love the night and I've always been someone who likes to stay up late. However, there's a difference between staying up all night because you've been listening to music and scribbling in your journal and staying up all night because you've been cleaning showers and carrying garbage bags out to a truck stop dumpster. When you're performing labor, you're forced to stay energized in a way that's different than when you're at home enjoying yourself. Regardless of what time the clock has struck, you can't go to sleep in the next hour. You need to stay fully alert and active, so you can fulfil your obligations and perform your tasks to the best of your ability. And when the eight-hour shift is over, I'm someone who needs to mentally reward myself in some way by relaxing and having fun. So, ultimately, I wasn't even going to bed shortly after the sun rose. I was going to bed several hours later, around the crack of noon.

Additionally, working overnight shift can alter your mental state in a way that's unpredictable and can be difficult to explain. The longer I worked overnight shift, the more I felt divorced from the world. I felt like a zombie who only really knew his fellow zombies at the truck stop. If a friend wanted to contact me, I was probably sleeping. And anyone who I used to interact with in my daily life at home or out in the world was now barely a part of it except on the weekend. I slept through prime-time TV and breaking news. I slept through life and I worked with the living dead – the Boiling Pan workers, a few truck drivers on the road, some local stoners with the munchies and my co-worker Sid.

I felt a camaraderie with Sid, my fellow zombie. Because it was overnight shift and there were barely any customers, he and I were the only people working in the Petrol store. He worked both the fuel desk and the cash register as I was the overnight shift porter. I was stuck with him while the world passed us by. Even if I had reasons to dislike him, it was almost like I had Stockholm Syndrome. I couldn't help but feel affection for him mixed in with the distain.

"That was cold, bro," Sid said.

"Thanks," I replied.

"But did you just say something about selling coke to truck drivers?" Sid inquired.

"Yeah, and I also rapped about chopping off a motherfucker's head with an axe. It's just a freestyle, dude. It's like a Twiztid song and not necessarily reality. And anyway, like I said in the rap, mind your bees wax!" I replied.

Sid laughed.

Sid's first name is Reggie, but everyone calls him by his middle name, "Sid." While Calvin may call himself the "office asshole," I'd say that Sid actually was the office asshole. He had the boss's back in all the worst ways.

I once had a conflict with a truck driver who was complaining about me, claiming I was being rude and belligerent when I was actually being as friendly and accommodating as possible. Sid saw the whole thing and knew I had done nothing wrong. I was hoping he'd talk, just say what happened and let Craig know that the customer's complaint had been senseless. However, he just stood there silently, like he was a deaf-ass motherfucker.

Sid was probably the biggest bootlicker at the truck stop. He was certainly an enemy of collective bargaining. We weren't allowed to discuss wages with each other, much less discuss wages collectively with management. Bootlicking Sid stood by this rule one hundred percent. He always said it wasn't his co-workers' business how much money he made, even though our income came from the same source. While working the overnight shift, Sid would sometimes come into work after drinking with his buddies at a nearby bar. Sid was an incompetent suck-up who pretended to be everyone's friend, but he really only cared about himself.

A historian once said, "socialism never took root in America because the poor see themselves not as an exploited proletariat, but as temporarily embarrassed millionaires." This quote is often misattributed to John Steinbeck but it was actually said by Ronald Wright. It's an accurate way to describe most of the employees at the truck stop but it's an especially accurate description of Sid.

Sid idolized famous rappers and the money they made. He wanted to be rich like Lil Wayne or Jay Z. Sid was a young, white man with rural, Midwestern roots. He talked about how "fools" in the city were always shooting each other and he was afraid to go there. He said any illegal immigrants working in the Boiling Pan kitchen should be deported. And he said Calvin would surely disagree with him about deporting these truck stop employees because they were "his kind," referring to the fact that they were Mexican immigrants.

Despite these prejudiced attitudes, Sid sure loved his mainstream, corporate rap music. He imitated how famous rappers talked, and he certainly admired their wealth and how they presumably started from the bottom. Perhaps making lots of money in the music industry was inspirational to Sid – even if he wasn't a rapper or a musician himself. Perhaps part of Sid believed he would one day be a millionaire or billionaire, I'm not entirely sure. However, I do know that "solidarity" was a four-letter word to Sid. And the idea of working-class unity was more of a foreign concept to him than the working-class foreigners who weren't "his kind."

After fiddling with his MP3 player, Sid put on another beat. Just as I started to rap another freestyle, my cell phone rang. My thoughts raced. Why is someone calling me after 3AM? I wasn't expecting a call in the middle of the night. I had to answer it.

Employees frequently slept on the couch in the break room, especially during overnight shift. There were surveillance cameras everywhere at the truck stop, including in the break room. However, management didn't really care about sleeping on your break. And they were unlikely to say anything about me and Sid talking to each other and having a good time instead of working – or at least not when it was the dead of night and there wasn't a customer in sight. However, pulling out my cell phone on the job is something I've had a stern talking to about on several occasions. Even if it was just to check the time, this was something I couldn't do on camera.

And for the record, management absolutely did watch the surveillance videos. Craig once asked me why I spat on the rug before I vacuumed it. He asked me this embarrassing question because he saw me doing this on camera.

In the middle of the freestyle rap, I stopped and said, "hold on, man. I gotta answer this."

Sid nodded. I walked to the bathroom – the only place where there are no surveillance cameras. By this time, my phone had stopped ringing, but I pulled it out and checked who it was.

It was an unknown caller. How peculiar. Perhaps I should just ignore this but it's 3AM and there honestly isn't much work to do right now. I walked from the bathroom into the large janitorial closet that's also where the porters talk to each other between shifts and get ready. It's a small room that contains a bulletin board, our Petrol smocks, work shoes and cleaning supplies. Some porters half-jokingly refer to this room as our "office."

I proceeded to call this unknown caller back. The phone almost went to voicemail before someone picked up. It was a woman. Her voice sounded pretty.

"Hello… Mitch?"

"Hi, who is this? You called?"

"Yes," she answered. "My bad. I'm a little drunk. We met at the Anti-Flag show last weekend."

That was a great show. I recognized Karen's voice now. I had smoked a joint with her in her car. When the bands played, she'd sung along to every word at the top of her lungs. Eventually, I'd done the same. I'd been very intoxicated by the end of the night and didn't even remember giving her my number, so this was a pleasant surprise.

"Oh, right. Karen! How goes it? I'm actually at work right now," I informed her.

"Really? Where ya work?" Karen inquired.

"A truck stop. I'm the maintenance guy, basically. Holt might be working here soon, too."

Holt had come to the show with me. He isn't a fan of punk music, but he'd accompanied me to the show because he likes to drink, and I had needed a friend. Holt doesn't really smoke either, so I'd been happy to find Karen. I hadn't wanted to get high alone. After smoking with Karen and her friend in her car, Holt and I had hung out with them for the rest of the concert.

"That's cool. Are you gonna live your life a slave?" Karen asked.

I awkwardly laughed and replied, "what?"

"You know, like the song," she clarified, giggling.

"Oh, right. 'When the cities burn down, we'll all keep warm,'" I said, quoting the Anti-Flag song she was referencing.

"Yeah, something like that. Fuck the system! Burn it down! We have nothing to lose but our chains." I thought about Karen's punk rock smile as I listened to her say this. Nonetheless, I wasn't sure if I could agree.

"I don't know if it's that simple." I said. "Good song, though!"

"What do you mean?" she asked.

"I mean, like… what would really happen if the workers seized the means of production?"

"What do you think? We'd have more freedom and happiness," Karen proclaimed.

CHAPTER 6
DIESEL DOCTRINE

My hours have been cut. After nearly three years of working full-time at this truck stop, the company has cut my hours. I was pissed. I had car payments, car insurance and a cell phone bill to pay. This is to say nothing of groceries and gasoline. I was once at forty hours, then they cut me down to thirty-two hours. Now I'm only working twenty-four hours and three days a week. Before I was full-time, but now I'm part-time.

They told me to blame ObamaCare. The party line at Petrol was that President Barack Obama was to blame. He's the reason a workforce that was once made up almost entirely of full-time employees was suddenly reduced to about 25% full-time employees. The people who run the company didn't want to pay for the new health benefits that the Affordable Care Act was requiring of full-time employees. They responded to this by making most of us part-time. This was a company-wide change in operation.

At my truck stop, I was surrounded by people who blamed our hours getting cut on Obama. Kelly in the restaurant told me, "I know you think it's Petrol, but it's really ObamaCare."

Yeah, like the President of the United States sent a memo to Petrol's corporate office to cut our hours. Smith, one of the porters, saw through the cloak of bullshit to a certain degree. He knew better than to blame Obama.

He said, "Obama gonna make it right. Obama gonna make it so everybody get ObamaCare, not just full-timers."

Calvin, the voice of reason, the face of Petrol and yet the opposite of everything I hated about Petrol at the same time, said, "Obama had good intentions, but he fucked up."

Me? I was just fucking pissed. Fuck the company, fuck the president, fuck the economy and most of all, fuck my bosses. Fuck Cindy and fuck the district manager too, whatever the hell his name is. I think it's Glen or some shit. But does it even matter? What does that clown even do for this truck stop other than wag his finger and get the metaphorical red carpet pulled out for him when he visits? As an employee on the bottom of the food chain, I do more to keep things running than management, who are just a bunch of parasites.

Cindy sits in her office all day fucking off while I'm literally cleaning the shit off the wall and providing customer service to truck drivers. And now management has the audacity to cut my hours like I'm just a robot they're dialing down and not a human being with thoughts, feelings and identity. Perhaps Karen was right about how the workers should own the means of production. This is how I've been repaid me after years of service during America's "Great Recession." I did my time and I worked my ass off, but no one gave a shit. Perhaps I wasn't a big enough suck-up.

A cashier named Dave recently transferred to another truck stop. He transferred with our old boss Craig to become a shift lead. I remember when Dave was the new guy and people at the fuel desk complained about his half-assed work. And yet, where was I? I was still a lowly porter, cleaning toilets while he gets to spend much of his time sitting in a comfy chair in front of his computer in the manager's office. There's no reason why I can't be a shift lead. I understand the culture of the place, I'm good with computers and quite frankly, I'm smarter than most or all the people here. Holt has said it before. He thinks it's ironic that the two of us are the smartest people at this place and yet we have low-level ranks.

It was 4:15 PM and Holt had finally arrived. He walked into the laundry room where I was folding towels. As soon as I saw him, I said, "dude, there's something I gotta tell you about."

"The world is coming to an end?"

I laughed and replied, "no, nothing that awesome. I'm thinking about transferring. I texted Craig and he said if I go over there, he'll give me the hours I need."

Holt hung up his leather jacket in the corner of the room and replied, "I don't want to be here."

"Yeah, I'm sick of the bullshit, but I honestly don't mind the job itself."

"Anyway," I continued. "I might do it. I might transfer. We'll see what happens. After today, I have four days in a row off. I've never had four days in a row off since I worked here. Hell, I used to get overtime and got to work six days a week, sometimes."

Holt nodded. "Yeah, I noticed that on the schedule." He looked grumpier than usual. He was always in a bad mood when working here, but he looked especially droopy in this moment.

"Are you hung over?" I asked.

"A little bit."

"Aw, shit… who'd ya go out with? And I wasn't invited?"

"The usual suspects. I didn't get back till past 4AM and I knew you had work in the morning."

"Oh, okay. Hold on. One second. Don't go anywhere."

"I'll be here," Holt said dryly.

I unplugged my phone charger and put it in my backpack. Then I walked down the hall to the break room and went inside. There was a container of leftover food from my lunch break. I pulled it out and stuffed it in my backpack. I ran downstairs and changed into my regular clothes. I walked to the restaurant to clock out, said hello to the night shift waitresses and then walked back upstairs. Holt was now in the middle of cleaning Shower Number 3.

I walked in and said, "a-yo, speaking of Craig, remember what he used to say when he was frustrated with an employee? 'It's not rocket science'? Well, duh. Of course it's not rocket science. Rocket science is logical and makes fucking sense. These methods are definitely not rocket science. This shit isn't logical and makes no sense at all. That's why we don't know to do it that way."

Holt chuckled and said, "yeah."

"Anyway," I continued. "I think I'm gonna write a short story about this place called 'Diesel Doctrine.' It'll be cathartic, you know? I got some proletariat rage bottled up. And I definitely need to let it out in some way.'"

Holt paused and thought about it. "Diesel Doctrine, eh? Well, working at a truck stop is a lot like joining a cult. Both are a small group of people who seem larger than their sheer numbers. Both are groups that would be viewed as collectively insane if the outside world had a peak of the inside."

I laughed. "I know, right? It was just supposed to be a catchy title. But I after I came up with the title, I got to thinking. What would the main tenets of Diesel Doctrine be? The first tenet of Diesel Doctrine is a high ingestion of caffeine —— whether it be Monster, the cheap off-brand energy drinks we sell, the pills by the cash register or 'extreme' Petrol coffee."

Holt laughed and said, "yeah, since workin' here, I've taken a lot more caffeine pills. What about how you gotta be a suck up to get ahead?"

"Yeah, the second tenet of Diesel Doctrine should be that work performance doesn't seem to matter a whole lot. Or even intelligence. It's the way you play the cards you've been given that determine your most success, nothing more, nothing less."

"And never steal cleaning supplies," Holt interjected.

"That's right!" I replied. "Never steal cleaning supplies."

"Like the device we use to fill up spray bottles at work. Never bring your own spray bottle, fill it up with glass cleaner and take it home."

"Nope, never, ever! Diesel Doctrine, motherfucker!"

"But anyway," I said, changing the subject, "in all seriousness, what might the third tenet of Diesel Doctrine be?"

"Be a snitch," Holt replied.

"Yep, tell the boss everything," I laughed.

Holt walked out of the shower room and I followed. He punched in the code and put the shower back in service. He then walked over to the next shower that needed to be cleaned. I followed behind him.

"Okay, let's be serious, not just sarcastic," I said. "What truly is the Diesel Doctrine? What is an unspoken rule about workin' at a truck stop? What is a defining characteristic of this subculture we are a part of?"

No one spoke for about twenty seconds.

Finally, Holt broke the silence. "Nothing. We clean the shit off toilets for less than ten bucks an hour. We're freakin' janitors and customer service attendants for truck drivers. Truck drivers are often fat from being on the road all the time and eating the unhealthy food we serve. They're weird as hell from having so little social interaction for long periods of time. We're expected to be 'day makers' 'cuz we're the only assholes these drivers have talked to in days. We're expected to sympathize with them, so corporate make us watch a Hallmark-ass video about a truck driver who is tryin' to make it home for his kid's basketball game.

"Management preaches to us about how we gotta make their days and be sympathetic. But why should we? I worked Christmas morning just like many truck drivers. They have a career and we work a dead-end, low-wage job. Ultimately, no one sympathizes with the poor truck driver earning more than double our income, and no porter is passionate about the work he or she does here. It's all a façade. It's all nonsense. It's all bullshit. It's all an illusion that you'd have to breathe in enough diesel exhaust to truly believe. What's so special about this place? Absolutely nothing. We've just been here so long, we make shit deeper than it actually is. A lot of motherfuckers are crazy here, and we can't help but laugh along with them and become one of them because we spend so much time here."

"But why are so many motherfuckers crazy here?" I asked.

"Because you gotta be crazy to successfully hold a job at a truck stop. There are so many other crappy, low wage jobs out there. Why stay at a truck stop if you don't secretly kinda like it? There's obviously something wrong with you if you work at this fucking place. And goddamn, if we're crazy then imagine how batshit insane the folks who run this company must be."

"I know, right?" I said. "There must be something in the water."

CHAPTER 7
THE CONCLUSION

"So, Calvin, how was Mexico?"

"It sucked, man. It's good to be home."

I smirked and signed the receipt to receive my employee discount for the energy drink I was purchasing.

"Home is where the heart is but home sucks, too. I'd rather be livin' in the city than down here," continued Calvin.

"Indeed," I replied. "We can't just hope for something better. We got to work for something better. Everyone here's got an asshole, and every asshole's got an excuse for why they've worked here for so long. We're failures of the American dream, I suppose. I'd like to say something more positive, like how there are better opportunities out there. But who the hell am I to preach when I'm still here at this fucking place just like you?"

Calvin smirked. "That's deep, man. You're so full of shit, but that's deep. I'll have to think about that the next time a dickhead truck driver is bitchin' at me about something outside of my control."

"Well," I said. "I'd hate to be even more full of shit, but to quote Rocky Balboa, 'If you stay in one place long enough, you become that place.'" I cracked open my energy drink, sipped it and laughed. "I call it 'Diesel Doctrine,' motherfucker."

Acknowledgments

Thanks to everyone who backed *Diesel Doctrine and the Temporarily Embarrassed Millionaires* on Kickstarter! This book wouldn't exist without you guys.

Deirdre Roberts
Larell Johnson
Matt Hoffman
Darius Payne
Ben Ferrari
Tim Rossi
Barbara Ann Siemens
Steve Aultz
Ryan Skelly
Christopher Wade
"Big Red"
Wolf Owczarek

Greg Mclemen
Alyssa Miller
Zachariah Gonzalez
Becky & Clyde Baggett
Lalinda De La Fuente
Ed Kolkebeck
DaiQuan Cain
Kendra Reinshagen
Sean Lowery
Shawn Pryor
"Geo"

Special thanks to **Lindsay Moore** for vigorously proofreading, editing and critiquing this book. I am immensely grateful for her fantastic work. She did more than just edit my syntax. This story wouldn't be as good as it is without her. Thanks to **Jorge Santiago Jr.** for designing the front and back covers and designing the interior of this book. He played a crucial role in putting together my book of poetry, *As the Moonlight Shines*, and he didn't let me down this time either. And thanks to **Ed Kolkebeck** for writing *Diesel Doctrine*'s Introduction. I'm glad I could count on you, homie.

Thanks to **Deirdre Roberts** for her generous Kickstarter pledge and her moral support for my writing. Thanks to **Kristin Palmer** for providing the prints I shipped to higher-level

Kickstarter backers. She painted a beautifully haunting illustration for my first book, *As the Moonlight Shines*, too. Thanks to the **unsung heroes** who made generous donations to *Diesel Doctrine's* Kickstarter, but didn't want to be listed here. And thanks to **Steve Aultz** for mentoring me and critiquing my writing through the years. He read an early draft of *Diesel Doctrine* and he made some suggestions that played a crucial role to how I wrote the story.

Finally, an extra special thanks to that fucking asshole **Greg Mclemen**. Once upon a time, he hired me to clean toilets at a shitty ass truck stop. And years later, in 2019, he made a very generous Kickstarter pledge and helped bring this book to life.

If I missed anyone, I apologize. You are appreciated, nonetheless.

About the Author

Nick Ulanowski is an aspiring journalist and the author of *As the Moonlight Shines*. When he isn't studying for exams, he's reading comic books and critiquing movies online. *Diesel Doctrine and the Temporarily Embarrassed Millionaires* is his second book, but it won't be his last. Be on the lookout for Nick Ulanowski the next time a news story breaks and a group of journalists exposes a corporate crime or government scandal.